The Four Clever Brothers

and other stories

Miles Kelly

First published in 2011 by Miles Kelly Publishing Ltd
Harding's Barn, Bardfield End Green, Thaxted, Essex, CM6 3PX, UK

Copyright © Miles Kelly Publishing Ltd 2011

This edition printed 2013

2 4 6 8 10 9 7 5 3

Publishing Director Belinda Gallagher

Creative Director Jo Cowan

Editor Amanda Askew

Senior Designer Joe Jones

Production Manager Elizabeth Collins

Reprographics Anthony Cambray, Stephan Davis, Lorraine King, Jennifer Hunt

Assets Lorraine King

ISBN 978-1-84810-501-0

Printed in China

British Library Cataloguing-in-Publication Data
A catalogue record for this book is available from the British Library

ACKNOWLEDGEMENTS
Artworks are from the Miles Kelly Artwork Bank

Every effort has been made to acknowledge the source and copyright holder of each picture.
Miles Kelly Publishing apologises for any unintentional errors or omissions.

Made with paper from a sustainable forest

www.mileskelly.net
info@mileskelly.net

www.factsforprojects.com

Contents

The Four Clever Brothers

By the Brothers Grimm

A POOR MAN ONCE SAID to his four sons, "Dear children, I have nothing to give you. You must go out into the wide world and try your luck. Begin by learning some craft or another, and see how you can get on."

So the brothers took their walking sticks in their hands, and their little bundles on their shoulders, and after bidding their father goodbye, went out of the gate together. When they had gone some way, they came to four crossways, each leading to a different country.

Then the eldest said, "Here we must part, but on this day in four years time we will come back to this spot, and in the meantime each must try to see what he can do for himself."

So each brother went his way, and as the eldest was hastening on he met a man, who asked him where he was going, and what he wanted.

"I am going to try my luck in the world, and should like to begin by learning some art or trade," answered he.

"Then," said the man, "Come with me, and I will teach you to become the most cunning thief that has ever been."

"No," said the other, "that is not an honest calling, and what can one look to earn but the gallows?"

"Oh!" said the man. "You need not fear the gallows, for I will only teach you to steal what will be fair game. I meddle with nothing but what no one else can get or care anything about."

So the young man agreed to follow his trade, and he soon showed himself so clever, that nothing could escape him that he had once set his mind upon.

The second brother also met a man, who, when he found out what he was setting out upon, asked him what craft he meant to follow.

"I do not know," said he.

"Then come with me, and be a stargazer. It is a noble art, for nothing can be hidden from you, when once you understand the stars." The plan pleased him much,

and he soon became such a skilful stargazer, that when he had served out his time, and wanted to leave his master, he gave him a glass, and said, "With this you can see all that is passing in the sky and on earth, and nothing can be hidden from you."

The third brother met a huntsman, who took him with him, and taught him so well about hunting, that he became very clever in the craft of the woods. When he left his master he gave him a bow, and said, "Whatever you shoot at with this bow you will be sure to hit."

The youngest brother likewise met a man who asked him what he wished to do. "Would not you like," said he, "to be a tailor?"

"Oh, no!" said the young man. "Sitting cross-legged from morning to night, working backwards and forwards with a needle, will never suit me."

"Oh!" answered the man. "That is not my sort of tailoring. Come with me, and you will learn quite another kind of craft from that."

Not knowing what better to do, he came into the plan, and learnt tailoring from the beginning. When he left his master, he gave him a needle, and said, "You can sew anything with this, be it as soft as an egg or as hard as steel, and the joint will be so fine that no seam will be seen."

After the space of four years, at the time agreed upon, the four brothers met at the four crossroads, and having welcomed each other, set off towards their father's home, where they told him all that had

happened to them, and how each had learned some craft.

Then, one day, as they were sitting before the house under a very high tree, the father said, "I should like to try what each of you can do in this way." So he looked up, and said to the second son, "At the top of this tree there is a chaffinch's nest, tell me how many eggs there are in it."

The stargazer took his glass, looked up, and said, "Five."

"Now," said the father to the eldest son, "take away the eggs without letting the bird that is sitting upon them know anything of what you are doing."

So the cunning thief climbed up the tree, and brought back to his father the five eggs from under the bird, and it never saw or felt what he was doing, but kept sitting at its ease.

Then the father took the eggs, and put one on each corner of the table, and the fifth in the middle, and said to the huntsman, "Cut all the eggs in two pieces at one shot." The huntsman took up his bow, and at one shot struck all the five eggs as his father wished.

"Now comes your turn," said he to the young tailor, "sew the eggs and the young birds in them together again, so neatly that the shot shall have done them no harm." Then the tailor took his needle, and sewed the eggs as he was told, and when he had done, the thief was sent to take them back to the nest, and put them under the bird without its knowing it. Then she went on sitting, and hatched them, and in a few days they crawled out, and had only a little red streak across their necks, where the tailor had sewn them together.

"Well done, sons!" said the old man. "You have made good use of your time, and learnt something worth knowing, but I am sure I do not know which ought to have the prize. I wish that a time might soon come for you to turn your skill to some account!"

Not long after this there was a great bustle in the country, for the king's daughter had been carried off by a mighty dragon, and the king mourned over his loss day and night, and made it known that whoever brought her back to him should have her for a wife. Then the four brothers said to each other, "Here is a chance for us, let us try what we can do."

And they agreed to see whether they could not set the princess free. "I will soon find out where she is," said the stargazer, as he looked through his glass, and he soon cried out, "I see her far off, sitting upon a rock in the sea, and I can spy the dragon close by, guarding her."

Then he went to the king, and asked for a ship for himself and his brothers, and they sailed together over the sea, till they came to the right place. There they found the princess sitting, as the stargazer had said, on the rock, and the dragon was lying asleep, with his head upon her lap. "I dare not shoot at him," said the huntsman, "for I should kill the princess also."

"Then I will try my skill," said the thief, and went and stole her away from under the dragon, so quietly that the beast did not know it, but went on snoring.

Then away they hastened with her, full of joy in their boat towards the ship, but soon came the dragon roaring behind them through the air, for it awoke and missed the princess. But when it got over the boat, and wanted to pounce upon them and carry off the princess, the huntsman took up his bow and shot it straight through the heart so that it fell down dead. They were still not safe, for it was such a great beast that in its fall it overset the boat, and they had to swim in the open sea upon a few planks. So the tailor took his needle, and with a few large stitches put some of the planks together, and he sat down upon these, and sailed about and gathered up all pieces of the boat, and then tacked them together so quickly that the boat was soon ready, and they then reached the ship and got home safely.

When they took the princess back to her father, there was great rejoicing, and he said to the four brothers, "One of you shall marry her, but you must settle among yourselves which it is to be." Then there arose a quarrel between them, and the stargazer said, "If I had not found the princess out, all your skill would have been of no use, therefore she ought to be mine."

"Your seeing her would have been of no use," said

the thief, "if I had not taken her away from the dragon, therefore she ought to be mine."

"No, she is mine," said the huntsman, "for if I had not killed the dragon, it would, after all, have torn you and the princess into pieces."

"And if I had not sewn the boat together again," said the tailor, "you would all have been drowned, therefore she is mine."

Then the king said, "Each of you is right, and as all cannot have the young lady, the best way is for neither of you to have her. The truth is, there is somebody she likes a great deal better. But to make up for your loss, I will give each of you half a kingdom." So the brothers agreed that this plan would be much better than either quarrelling or marrying a lady who had no mind to have them. And the king then gave to each half a kingdom, as he had said, and they lived very happily the rest of their days. They took good care of their father, and somebody took better care of the young lady, than to let either the dragon or one of the craftsmen have her again.

I Wonder

By Kate Douglas Wiggin

ONCE UPON A TIME there was a man who had three sons – Peter, Paul, and the least of all, whom they called Youngling. I can't say the man had anything more than these three sons, for he hadn't one penny to rub against another. He told the lads, over and over again, that they must go out into the world and try to earn their bread, for at home there was nothing to be looked for but starving to death.

Now nearby the man's cottage was the king's palace, and, you must know, just against the windows a great oak had sprung up, which was so stout and tall that it took away all the light. The king had said he would give untold treasure to the man who could fell the oak,

but no one was man enough for that, for as soon as one chip of the oak's trunk flew off, two grew in its stead.

A well, too, the king desired, which was to hold water for the whole year, for all his neighbours had wells, but he hadn't any, and that he thought a shame. So the king said he would give both money and goods to anyone who could dig him such a well as would hold water for a whole year round, but no one could do it, for the palace lay high, high up on a hill, and they could only dig a few inches before they came upon rock.

But, as the king had set his heart on having these two things done, he had it given out far and wide, in all the churches of his dominion, that he who could fell the big oak in the king's courtyard, and get him a well that would hold water the whole year round, should have the princess and half the kingdom.

Well! You may easily know there was many a man who came to try his luck, but all their hacking and hewing, all their digging and delving, were of no avail. The oak grew taller and stouter at every stroke, and the rock grew no softer.

So one day the three brothers thought they'd set off and try, too, and their father hadn't a word against it, for, even if they didn't get the princess and half the kingdom, it might happen that they would get a place somewhere with a good master, and that was all he wanted. So when the brothers said they thought of going to the palace, their father said "Yes" at once, and Peter, Paul and Youngling went off from their home.

They had not gone far before they came to a fir wood, and up along one side of it rose a steep hillside, and as they went, they heard something hewing and hacking away up on the hill among the trees.

"I wonder now what it is that is hewing away up yonder?" said Youngling.

"You are always so clever with your wonderings," said Peter and Paul, both at once. "What wonder is it, pray, that a woodcutter should stand and hack up on a hillside?"

"Still, I'd like to see what it is, after all," said Youngling, and up he went.

"Oh, if you're such a child, it'll do you good to go and take a lesson," cried out his brothers after him.

But Youngling didn't care for what they said, he climbed the steep hillside towards where the noise came, and when he reached the place, what do you think he saw?

Why, an axe that stood there hacking and hewing, all by itself, at the trunk of a fir tree.

"Good day," said Youngling. "So you stand here all alone and hew, do you?"

"Yes, here I've stood and hewed and hacked a long, long time, waiting for you, my lad," said the axe.

"Well, here I am at last," said Youngling, as he took the axe, pulled it off its haft, and stuffed both head and haft into his wallet.

So when he climbed down again to his brothers, they began to jeer and laugh at him.

"And now, what funny thing was it you saw up on the hillside?" they said.

"Oh, it was only an axe we heard," said Youngling. When they had gone a bit farther they heard something digging and shovelling.

"I wonder, now," said Youngling, "what it is digging and shovelling up yonder at the top of the rock?"

"Ah, you're always so clever with your wonderings," said Peter and Paul again, "as if you'd never heard a woodpecker hacking and pecking at a hollow tree."

"Well, well," said Youngling, "I think it would be a piece of fun just to see what it really is."

And so off he set to climb the rock, while the others laughed and made fun of him. But he didn't care a bit for that. Up he clambered, and when he got near the top, what do you think he saw? Why, a spade that stood there digging and delving.

"Good day," said Youngling. "So you stand here all alone, and dig and delve?"

"Yes, that's what I do," said the spade, "and that's what I've done this many a long day, waiting for you, my lad."

"Well, here I am," said Youngling again, as he took the spade and knocked off its handle, and put it into his wallet, and then he climbed down again to his brothers.

"Well, what was it, so strange and rare," said Peter and Paul, "that you saw up there at the top of the rock?"

"Oh," said Youngling, "nothing more than a spade, that was what we heard."

So they went on again a good bit, till they came to a brook. They were thirsty after their long walk, and so they sat beside the brook to have a drink.

"I have a great fancy to see where this brook comes from," said Youngling.

So up alongside the brook he went, in spite of all that his brothers shouted after him. Nothing could stop him. On he went. And as he went up and up, the brook grew smaller and smaller, and at last, a little way farther on, what do you think he saw? Why, a great walnut, and out of that the water trickled.

"Good day," said Youngling again. "So you lie here and trickle, and run down all alone?"

"Yes, I do," said the walnut "and here have I trickled and run this many a long day, waiting for you, my lad."

"Well, here I am," said Youngling, as he took a lump of moss and plugged up the hole, so that the water wouldn't run out. Then he put the walnut into his wallet, and ran down to his brothers.

"Well," said Peter and Paul, "have you found where the water comes from? A rare sight it must have been!"

"Oh, after all, it was only a hole it ran out of," said Youngling, and the others laughed and made game of him again, but Youngling didn't mind that a bit.

So when they had gone a little farther, they came to the king's palace, but as every man in the kingdom had heard that he might win the princess and half the realm, if he could only fell the big oak and dig the king's well, so many had come to try their luck that the oak was now twice as stout and big as it had been at first, for you will remember that two chips grew for every one they hewed out with their axes.

So the king had now laid it down as a punishment that if anyone tried and couldn't fell the oak, he should be put on a barren island, and both his ears were to be clipped off. But the two brothers didn't let themselves be frightened by this threat, they were quite sure they could fell the oak, and Peter, as he was the eldest, was to try his hand first, but it went with him as with all the rest who had hewn at the oak – for every chip

he cut two grew in its place. So the king's men seized him, and clipped off both his ears, and put him out on the island.

Now Paul was to try his luck, but he fared just the same. When he had hewn two or three strokes, they began to see the oak grow, and so the king's men seized him, too, and clipped his ears, and put him out on the island, and they clipped his ears closer, because they said he ought to have taken a lesson from his brother.

So now Youngling was to try.

"If you want to look like a marked sheep, we're quite ready to clip your ears at once, and then you'll save yourself some trouble," said the king, for he was angry with him for his brothers' sake.

"Well, I'd just like to try first," said Youngling, and so he was given permission. Then he took his axe out of his wallet and fitted it to its handle.

"Hew away!" said he to his axe, and away it hewed, making the chips fly again, so that it wasn't long before down came the oak.

When that was done, Youngling pulled out his spade and fitted it to its handle.

"Dig away!" said he to his spade, and so the spade began to dig and delve till the earth and rock flew out in splinters, and he soon had the well deep enough, you may believe.

And when he had got it as big and deep as he chose, Youngling took out his walnut and laid it in one corner of the well, and pulled the plug of moss out.

"Trickle and run," said Youngling, and so the nut trickled and ran till the water gushed out of the hole in a stream, and in a short time the well was full.

So as Youngling had felled the oak that shaded the king's palace, and dug a well in the palace yard, he got the princess and half the kingdom, as the king had said, but it was lucky for Peter and Paul that they had lost their ears, else they might have grown tired of hearing how everyone said each hour of the day, "Well, after all, Youngling wasn't so much out of his mind when he took to wondering."

The Wise Girl

By Katharine Pyle

THERE WAS ONCE A GIRL who was wiser than the king and all his councillors – there never was anything like it. Her father was so proud of her that he boasted about her cleverness at home and abroad. He could not keep his tongue still about it. One day he was boasting to one of his neighbours, and he said, "The girl is so clever that not even the king could ask her a question she couldn't answer, or read her a riddle she couldn't unravel."

Now it so chanced the king was sitting at a window nearby, and he overheard what the girl's father was saying. The next day he sent for the man to come before him.

"I hear you have a daughter who is so clever that no one in the kingdom can equal her, and is that so?" asked the king.

Yes, the man said, it was no more than the truth. Too much could not be said of her wit and cleverness.

That was well, and the king was glad to hear it. He had thirty eggs, they were fresh and good, but it would take a clever person to hatch chickens out of them. He then bade his chancellor get the eggs and give them to the man.

"Take these home to your daughter," said the king, "and bid her hatch them out for me. If she succeeds she shall have a bag of money for her pains, but if she fails you shall be beaten as a vain boaster."

The man was troubled when he heard this. Still his daughter was so clever he was almost sure she could hatch out the eggs. He carried them home to her and told her exactly what the king had said. It did not take the girl long to find out that the eggs had been boiled.

When she told her father, he made a great to-do. That was a pretty trick for the king to have played upon him. Now he would have to take a beating and all the neighbours would hear about it. Would to heaven he had never had a daughter at all if that was what came of it.

The girl, however, told him to be of good cheer. "Go to bed and sleep quietly," said she. "I will think of some way out of the trouble. No harm shall come to you, even if I have to go to the palace myself and take the beating in your place."

The next day the girl gave her father a bag of boiled beans and told him to take them out to a certain place where the king rode by every day. "Wait until you see him coming," said she, "and then begin to sow the beans." At the same time he was to call out so loudly that the king could not help but hear him.

The man took the bag of beans and went out to the field his daughter had spoken of. He waited until he saw the king coming, and then he began to sow the beans, and at the same time to cry aloud, "Come sun, come rain! Heaven grant that these boiled beans may yield me a good crop."

The king was surprised that any one should be so stupid as to think boiled beans would grow and yield a crop. He did not recognize the man, for he had only seen him once, and he stopped his horse to speak to him. "My poor man," said he, "how can you expect boiled beans to grow? Do you not know that is impossible?"

"Whatever the king commands should be possible,"

answered the man, "and if chickens can hatch from boiled eggs why should not boiled beans yield a crop?"

When the king heard this he looked at the man more closely, and then he recognized him as the father of the clever daughter.

"You have indeed a clever daughter," said he. "Take your beans home and bring me back the eggs."

The man was glad when he heard that, and made

haste to obey. He carried the beans home then took the eggs and brought them back to the palace.

After the king had received the eggs he gave the man a handful of flax. "Take this to your daughter," he said, "and bid her make for me a full set of sails for a large ship. If she does this she shall receive half of my kingdom, but if she fails, you shall have a beating."

The man returned home lamenting his hard lot.

"What is the matter?" asked his daughter. "Has the king set another task that I must do?"

Yes, that he had – her father showed her the flax the king had sent her and gave her the message.

"Do not be troubled," said the girl. "No harm shall come to you. Go to bed and tomorrow I will send the king an answer that will satisfy him."

The man believed what his daughter said. He went to bed and slept quietly.

The next day, the girl gave her father a small piece of wood. "Carry this to the king," said she. "Tell him I am ready, but first let him make me a large ship out of this wood so that I may fit the sails to it."

The father did as the girl said, and the king was surprised at the cleverness of the girl.

"That is all very well," said he, "and I will excuse her from this task. Here is a glass mug. Take it home to your clever daughter. Tell her it is my command that she dip out the waters from the seabed so that I can ride over the bottom dry. If she does this, I will take her for my wife, but if she fails you shall be beaten."

The man took the mug and hastened home, weeping aloud and bemoaning his fate.

"Well, and what is it?" asked his daughter. "What does the king demand of me now?"

The man gave her the glass mug and told her what the king had said.

"Do not be troubled," said the girl. "Go to bed and sleep in peace. You shall not be beaten, and soon I shall be reigning as queen over all this land."

He trusted her, so went to bed and dreamed he saw her sitting by the king wearing a crown.

The next morning the girl gave her father a bunch of wool. "Take this to the king," she said. "Tell him that I am willing to dip the sea dry, but first, with this wool, let him stop up all the rivers that flow into the ocean."

The man did exactly as his daughter instructed him. He took the wool to the king and repeated what she had said word for word.

Then the king saw that the girl was indeed a clever one, and he sent for her to come before him.

She came just as she was, in her homespun dress

and her rough shoes and with a cap on her head, but for all her mean clothing, she was as pretty and fine as a flower, and the king was not slow to see it. Still he wanted to make sure for himself that she was as clever as her messages had been.

"Tell me," said he, "what sound can be heard the farthest throughout the world?"

"The thunder that echoes through heaven and earth," answered the girl, "and your own royal commands that go from lip to lip."

The king was so well satisfied with the way the girl answered that he no longer hesitated, he was determined that she should be his queen, and that they should be married at once.

The girl had something to say to this, however. "I am but a poor girl," said she, "and my ways are not your ways. It may well be that you will tire of me and send me back to my father's house to live. Promise that if this should happen, you will allow me to take the thing that has grown most precious to me."

The king was willing to agree to this. Then she and the king were married with the greatest magnificence, and she came to live in the palace.

Now after the girl became queen, she would wear nothing but magnificent robes and jewels and ornaments, for that seemed to her only right and proper for a queen. But the king, who was of a very jealous nature, thought his wife did not care at all for him, but only for the fine things that he could give her.

One day the king and queen were to ride abroad together, and the queen spent so much time in dressing herself that the king was kept waiting, and he became very angry. When she appeared before him, he would not even look at her. "You care nothing for me, but only for the jewels and fine clothes you wear!" he cried. "Take with you those that are the most precious to you, as I promised you, and return to your father's house. I will no longer have a wife who cares only for my possessions and not at all for me."

Very well, the girl was willing to go. "And I will be happier in my father's house than I was when I first met you," said she. Nevertheless she begged that she might spend one more night in the palace, and that she and the king might sup together once again before she returned home.

So he and his wife supped together that evening and when the king was not looking, she put a sleeping potion in the cup and gave it to him to drink. He drank it to the very last drop, suspecting nothing, but soon after he sank down among the cushions in a deep

sleep. Then the queen ordered him to be carried to her father's house and laid in the bed there.

When the king awoke, he was surprised to find himself in the peasant's cottage. The girl came to the bedside, dressed in common clothes.

"What means this?" said the king.

"My dear husband," said the girl, "your promise was that I might carry with me the thing that had become most precious to me in the castle. That is you."

The king could no longer feel angry. They returned to the palace, and from then on, lived together happily.

Hans in Luck

By Joseph Jacobs

SOME MEN ARE BORN to good luck – all they do or try to do comes right and all that falls to them is gain, all their geese are swans and all their cards are trumps. Toss them which way you will, they will always, like poor puss, alight upon their legs, and only move on so much the faster. The world may very likely not always think of them as they think of themselves, but what care they for the world? What can it know about the matter?

One of these lucky beings was neighbour Hans. Seven years he had worked hard for his master. At last he said, "Master, my time is up, I must go home and see my poor mother once more – so pray pay me my

wages and let me go." And the master said, "You have been a faithful servant, Hans, so your pay shall be handsome." He gave him a lump of silver as big as his head.

Hans took out his handkerchief, put the piece of silver into it, threw it over his shoulder, and jogged off on his road homewards. As he went lazily on, dragging one foot after another, a man came in sight, trotting gaily along on a capital horse. "Ah!" said Hans aloud. "What a fine thing it is to ride on horseback! There he sits as easy and happy as if he was at home, in the chair by his fireside, he trips against no stones, saves shoe leather, and gets on he hardly knows how."

Hans did not speak quietly, so the horseman heard it all, and said, "Well, friend, why do you go on

foot then?"

"Ah!" said he, "I have this load to carry. To be sure it is silver, but it is so heavy that I can't hold up my head, and you must know it hurts my shoulder badly."

"What do you say of making an exchange?" said the horseman. "I will give you my horse, and you shall give me the silver, which will save you a great deal of trouble in carrying such a heavy load about with you."

"With all my heart," said Hans, "but as you are so kind to me, I must tell you one thing – you will have a weary task to draw that silver about with you." However, the horseman got off, took the silver, helped Hans up, gave him the bridle into one hand and the whip into the other, and said, "When you want to go very fast, smack your lips loudly together, and cry 'Jip!'"

Hans was delighted as he sat on the horse, drew himself up, squared his elbows, turned out his toes, cracked his whip and rode merrily off, one minute whistling a merry tune, and another singing.

After a time he thought he should like to go a little faster, so he smacked his lips and cried, "Jip!" Away went the horse full gallop, and before Hans knew what he was about, he was thrown off, and lay on his back by the roadside. His horse would have run off, if a shepherd who was coming by, driving a cow, had not

stopped it. Hans soon came to himself, and got upon his legs again, sadly vexed, and said to the shepherd, "This riding is no joke, when a man has the luck to get upon a beast like this that stumbles and flings him off as if it would break his neck. However, I'm off now once and for all, I like your cow now a great deal better than this smart beast that played me this trick, and has spoiled my best coat, you see, in this puddle, which, by the by, smells not very like a nosegay. One can walk along at one's leisure behind that cow – keep good company, and have milk, butter, and cheese, every day, into the bargain. What would I give to have such a prize!"

"Well," said the shepherd, "if you are so fond of her, I will change my cow for your horse, I like to do good to my neighbours, even though I lose by it myself."

"Done!" said Hans, merrily. 'What a noble heart that good man has!' thought he. Then the shepherd jumped upon the horse, wished Hans and the cow good morning, and away he rode.

Hans brushed his coat, wiped his face and hands, rested a while, and then drove off his cow quietly, and thought his bargain a very lucky one. "If I have only a piece of bread (and I shall always be able to get that) I can, whenever I like, eat my butter and cheese with it, and when I am thirsty I can milk my cow and drink the milk. What more can I wish for?"

When he came to an inn, he halted, ate up all his bread, and gave away his last penny for a glass of beer. When he had rested himself he set off again, driving his cow towards his mother's village. But the heat grew greater as soon as noon came on, till at last, as he found himself on a wide heath that would take him more than an hour to cross, he began to feel so hot and parched that his tongue stuck to the roof of his mouth. 'I can find a cure for this,' thought he, 'now I will milk my cow and quench my thirst.' So he tied her to the stump of a tree, and held his leathern cap to milk into, but not a drop was to be had. Who would have thought that this cow, which was to bring him milk and butter and cheese, was all that time utterly dry? Hans had not thought of looking to that.

While he was trying his luck in milking, and managing the matter very clumsily, the uneasy beast began to think him very troublesome, and at last gave him such a kick on the head as knocked him down. And there he lay a long while senseless. Luckily a butcher soon came by, driving a pig in a wheelbarrow.

"What is the matter with you, my man?" said the butcher, as he helped him up. Hans told him what had

happened, how he was dry and wanted to milk his cow, but found the cow was dry too. Then the butcher gave him a flask of ale, saying, "There, drink and refresh yourself, your cow will give you no milk. Don't you see she is old, good for nothing but the slaughterhouse?"

"Alas, alas!" said Hans, "Who would have thought it? What a shame to take my horse and give me only a dry cow! If I kill her, what will she be good for? I hate beef, it is not tender enough for me. If it were a pig now – like that fat gentleman you are driving along at his ease – one could do something with it. It would at any rate make sausages."

"Well," said the butcher, "I don't like to say no, when one is asked to do a neighbourly thing. To please you I will change, and give you my fine fat pig for the cow."

"Heaven reward you for your kindness and self-denial!" said Hans, as he gave the butcher the cow, and taking the pig off the wheelbarrow, drove it away, holding it by the string that was tied to its leg.

So on he jogged, and all seemed now to go right with him – he had met with some misfortunes, to be sure, but he was now well repaid for all. How could it be otherwise with such a travelling companion as he had at last got?

The next man he met was a countryman carrying a

fine white goose. The countryman stopped to ask what was the time. This led to further chat, and Hans told him all his luck, how he had so many good bargains,

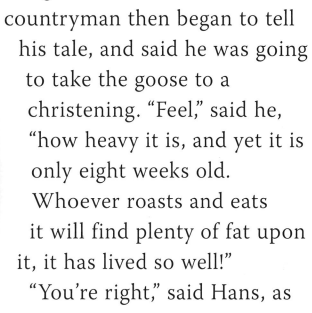

and how all the world went gay and smiling with him. The countryman then began to tell his tale, and said he was going to take the goose to a christening. "Feel," said he, "how heavy it is, and yet it is only eight weeks old. Whoever roasts and eats it will find plenty of fat upon it, it has lived so well!"

"You're right," said Hans, as he weighed it in his hand, "but if you talk of fat, my pig is no trifle."

The countryman began to look grave, and shook his head. "Listen!" said he, "My worthy friend, you seem a good sort of fellow, so I can't help doing you a kind turn. Your pig may get you into a scrape. In the village I just came from, the squire has had a pig stolen out of his sty. I was dreadfully afraid when I saw you that you had got the squire's pig. If you have, and they catch you, it will be bad for you. The least they will do will

be to throw you into the horse pond. Can you swim?"

Poor Hans was greatly frightened. "Good man," cried he, "pray get me out of this. I know nothing of where the pig was either bred or born, but he may have been the squire's for all I can tell – you know this country better than I do, take my pig and give me the goose."

"I ought to have something into the bargain," said the countryman, "give a fat goose for a pig, indeed! 'Tis not everyone would do so much for you as that. However, I will not be hard upon you, as you are in trouble." Then he took the string in his hand, and drove off the pig by a side path, while Hans went on the way homewards, free from care. 'After all,' thought he, 'that chap is pretty well taken in. I don't care whose pig it is, but wherever it came from it has been a very good friend to me. I have much the best of the bargain. First there will be a capital roast, then the fat will find me in goose grease for six months, and then there are all the beautiful white feathers. I will put them into my pillow, and then I am sure I shall sleep soundly.'

As he came to the next village, he saw a scissor-grinder with his wheel, working and singing.

Hans stood looking on for a while, and at last said, "You must be well off, master grinder! You seem so happy at your work."

"Yes," said the other, "mine is a golden trade, a good grinder never puts his hand into his pocket without finding money in it – but where did you get that beautiful goose?"

"I did not buy it, I gave a pig for it."

"And where did you get the pig?"

"I gave a cow for it."

"And the cow?"

"I gave a horse for it."

"And the horse?"

"I gave a lump of silver as big as my head for it."

"And the silver?"

"Oh! I worked hard for that seven long years."

"You have done well in the world," said the grinder, "now if you could find money in your pocket whenever you put your hand in it, your fortune would be made."

"Very true – but how is that to be managed?"

"How? Why, you must turn grinder like myself, said the other, you only want a grindstone, the rest will come of itself. Here is one that is but little the worse for wear, I would not ask more than the value of your goose for it – will you buy?"

"I should be the happiest man in the world, if I could have money whenever I put my hand in my pocket – what could I want more? There's the goose."

"Now," said the grinder, as he gave him a common rough stone that lay by his side, "this is a most capital stone, do but work it well enough, and you can make an old nail cut with it."

Hans took the stone, and went his way with a light heart, his eyes sparkled for joy, and he said to himself, 'Surely I must have been born in a lucky hour, everything I could want or wish for comes of itself. People are so kind – they think I do them a favour in letting them make me rich, and giving me bargains.'

At last he could go no farther, for the stone tired him sadly, and he dragged himself to the side of a river, that he might take a drink of water, and rest a while. So he laid the stone carefully by his side on the bank – but, as he stooped down to drink, he forgot it, pushed it a little, and down it rolled, plump into the stream.

For a while he watched it sinking in the deep, clear water, then sprang up and danced for joy, and thanked heaven for its kindness in taking away the heavy stone.

"Nobody was ever so lucky as I." Then he walked on till he reached his mother's house, and told her how easy the road to good luck was.